Thomas MacKellar

Hymns and a few Metrical Psalms

Thomas MacKellar

Hymns and a few Metrical Psalms

ISBN/EAN: 9783744779265

Printed in Europe, USA, Canada, Australia, Japan

Cover: Foto ©Andreas Hilbeck / pixelio.de

More available books at **www.hansebooks.com**

HYMNS

AND A FEW

METRICAL PSALMS

BY

THOMAS MACKELLAR.

Speaking to yourselves in psalms and hymns and spiritual songs,
singing and making melody with your heart to the Lord.
Eph. v. 19.

PHILADELPHIA:

PORTER & COATES.

1883.

PREFACE.

SOME of the hymns in this volume were written before a busy life had passed its noontide: others when the rays of the westering sun were falling slantwise. The latest were the outcome (as well as the alleviation) of times of anguish and bereavement.

A few of the earlier pieces have come into use in various hymnals. All that may be deemed fitting are at the service of the church.

T. McK.

GERMANTOWN, PA.
April, 1883.

1*

First Lines.

Laus Deo.

High and mighty God and Saviour!
   In the earth thy will be done:
Hallowed be thy Name forever,
   Holy Father, Holy Son,
     Holy Spirit!
    Lord Jehovah!
   Glory be to Thee alone.

HYMNS.

I. . . . . 8, 5.

A multitude of the heavenly host praising God, and saying, Glory to
God in the highest.—Luke ii. 13, 14.

I.

GLORY to God in the highest!
The day of all days
Awakens our praise,—
The thrice-blessed morn
When Jesus was born,—
The name that the church glorifieth:
Glory to God!
Glory to God!
Glory to God in the highest!

II.

Glory to God in the highest!
Let heaven resound
To its uttermost bound
With anthems of praise
Both now and always,

While seraph to seraph replieth,
　　Glory to God!
　　Glory to God!
Glory to God in the highest!

III.

Glory to God in the highest!
　　Let earth, with its hills,
　　Its valleys and rills,
　　Re-echo his praise
　　Both now and always,
While mountain to mountain-top crieth,
　　Glory to God!
　　Glory to God!
Glory to God in the highest!

IV.

Glory to God in the highest!
　　His goodwill and peace
　　To men will not cease:
　　The church lifts her voice
　　While angels rejoice,
And her song with the seraphim's vieth:
　　Glory to God!
　　Glory to God!
Glory to God in the highest!

V.

Glory to God in the highest!
The bountiful Lord,—
The Father, the Word,
The Spirit,—whose praise
Both now and always
On the wings of infinity flieth:
Glory to God!
Glory to God!
Glory to God in the highest!

1881.

II. . . . . 7's.

I laid me down and slept; I awaked; for the Lord sustained me.
Ps. iii. 5.

I.

DAY is breaking in the sky;
    Restful night has pass'd away:
Now I lift my early cry,
    Lead thy servant, Lord, to-day.

II.

Jesus, Master! forth I go,
    Taking up my 'custom'd task:
Teach me what I need to know,—
    Give me what I ought to ask.

III.

I see not the way before,
    But I go at thy command,
Entering gladly duty's door,
    Led by thy directing hand.

IV.

Take away my sin and guilt,
    Make me whiter than the snow:
Be my will just what Thou wilt,
    Asking not, Why is it so?

V.

May my soul, impell'd by love,
    Do whate'er thy Spirit saith,
That my life this day may prove,
    Through thy grace, the power of faith.

VI.

Glory to Thee evermore!
    Glory in the uttermost!
Heaven and earth thy name adore,
    Father, Son, and Holy Ghost.

1881.

III. . . . . C. M.

Yea, thou shalt lie down, and thy sleep shall be sweet.—Prov. iii. 24.

I.

UPON the pillow of Thy love
My weary head I lay,
Assured that watchers from above
Will round about me stay.

II.

The weanéd child, subdued and still,
Sleeps on its mother's breast;
So I, submissive to thy will,
Lean on thy strength for rest.

III.

The sighs, and tears, and agony
That marr'd the hours of day,
Subside as tempests on the sea
In silence die away.

IV.

The restful peace of answer'd prayer
    Is in my chasten'd heart:
My fears, my sorrows, and my care
    At thy command depart.

V.

O Lord, my God, my strength, my hope,
    In thee I find repose:
Vouchsafe my grateful eyes shall ope
    As softly as they close.

1881.

IV. . . . . C. M.

The way of man is not in himself: it is not in man that walketh
to direct his steps.—Jer. x. 23.

I.

I WOULD I were content to be
Just as my Lord shall will,
So I with cheerful constancy
His purpose may fulfil.

II.

O may I be content to lay
My hourly griefs and cares
Upon His arm that every day
His children's burden bears:

III.

Nor proudly strive to carry part
And leave to Him the rest,
So losing comfort of the heart
And healing of the breast.

IV.

Though I should ask the Lord to show
   Some greater things to do,
May I be ever quick to go
   On humble errands too:

V.

To run in haste, or waiting stand,
   Content to go or stay,
While watching for his guiding hand
   To point the fitting way.

VI.

Whatever work the day shall bring,
   May I set Thee before,
And give to Thee, O Christ, my King,
   The glory evermore.

1861.

V. . . . . C. M.

It shall come to pass, that at evening time it shall be light.
Zech. xiv. 7.

I.

B E not disquieted, my soul!
  'Tis grace that moves the Power
Whose hand thy destinies control
  In every varying hour.

II.

When sorrows fall, he wraps the heart
  The closer in his love:
If here he takes away a part,
  He'll give thee all above.

III.

Why tremble when thy God shall lay
  A shadow on thy path?
Not e'en the dark, distressful day
  Portends a night of wrath.

IV.

The heavy clouds that, dark and dun,
    Thine upward pathway hide,
Shall blaze with glory when the sun
    Goes down at eventide.

V.

And light from God's abiding-place
  · Shall fix the raptured eye,
The light of love in Jesus' face,
    To welcome thee on high.

1881.

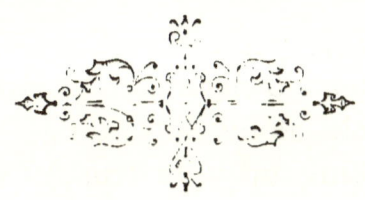

VI. . . . . 8, 7, 4.

Cast thy burden upon the Lord, and he shall sustain thee.—Ps. lv. 22.

I.

O THE blessedness of leaning
    On a strength beyond thine own!
O the fulness of the meaning—
    O the sweetness of the tone—
        Cast thy burden
    On thy loving Lord alone.

II.

Often weary, yet contending,—
    Beaten down, again to rise,—
On his help alone depending,
    Looking up with trustful eyes,—
        Cast thy burden
    On the arm that built the skies.

III.

Take his easy yoke upon thee,
    Lowly be like him in heart:

Child, it was his love that won thee,
    Will he bid thee now depart
        With thy burden,
    When thy soul is full of smart?

IV.

Long ago the word was written,—
    Word to generations blest,—
Hear it, children sorely smitten,
    Hear it, ye of troubled breast,—
        Cast thy burden
    On the Lord: he'll give thee rest.

1881.

VII. . . . . C. M.

When my spirit was overwhelmed within me, then thou knewest my path.—Ps. cxlii. 3.

I.

THOUGH darkness turn the skies to night,
  Though sorrows fill the air,
Nor moon nor stars my pathway light,
  Yet thou art with me there.

II.

I cannot see thee, but I know
  A stronger arm than mine
Upholds me in the time of woe,—
  Jesus! that arm is thine.

III.

Though words may fail when I would pray,
  And mute I lift my hands,
Thou hearest what I cannot say,
  And Gabriel near me stands.

IV.

A just God and a Saviour, thou
    Art full of love and grace:
Before thy majesty I bow
    With glad and trustful face.

V.

Thy sovereign grace gives sweet relief,
    Dispelling faithless gloom,
And the dark chamber of my grief
    Becomes a sunny room.

1881.

VIII. . . . . C. M.

I will be with thee: I will not fail thee, nor forsake thee.
Josh. i. 5.

I.

WHAT though the way be storm-begirt,
    If Jesus lead thee on!
Thou shalt not suffer loss or hurt,
    Nor walk the path alone.

II.

Must thou do battle on the way?
    The arm of God is thine:
Does he unprop thine earthly stay?
    Upon that arm recline.

III.

Has he not pledged his word to save?
    Will he himself deny?
Will he not hold thee fast who gave
    His Son for thee to die?

IV.

The Father chasteneth whom he will,
   And some he wills to spare;
But not the less he loveth still
   The souls that meekly bear.

V.

O Lord, my timorous heart control;
   Forgive my doubt and sin :
Open the windows of my soul
   And let thy sunlight in.

1861.

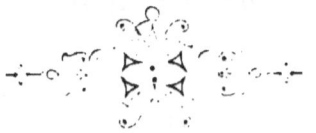

IX. . . . . 8, 7.

Behold the birds of the heaven, that then sow not, neither do then reap, nor gather into barns; and your heavenly Father feedeth them. Be not therefore anxious for the morrow: for the morrow will be anxious for itself.—Matt. vi. 26, 34.

I.

BE not anxious for the morrow,
　Let the morrow have its cares:
Soul, be not forecasting sorrow;
　Grace is given to him who bears
Crosses that he does not borrow:
　God controls the unawares.

II.

Neither sowing, neither reaping,
　Gathering not to store away,
Birds are in the Father's keeping,—
　Cares he not when children pray?
Why then, faithless, sighing, weeping,
　Doubt him for the coming day?

III.

Lilies, toiling not nor spinning,
    Gleam in robes beyond compare :
Never king from time's beginning
    Had such glorious dress to wear :
Souls that cost his life in winning
    Christ will keep with loving care.

1861.

X. . . . . 8, 7, 4.

Blessed are those servants whom the Lord when he cometh shall find
watching.—Luke xii. 37.

Watch ye, stand fast in the faith, quit you like men, be strong.
1 Cor. xvi. 13.

I.

WATCHERS call'd to work for Jesus,
    To the glory of his name,
In the field where'er he pleases
    Our glad services to claim,—
        Ever ready!
    This our watchword and our aim.

II.

Watching for the revelation
    Of his glory and his grace,
When the power of his salvation
    Shall subdue earth's rebel race,—
        Always watching,
    Always standing in our place.

III.

Watching for the coming morning,
  Resting in the Saviour's might,
Even now we see its dawning,
    See the shafts of heavenly light
      Pierce the darkness
    That enwrapt the world in night.

IV.

Watching while our hands are doing;
  Loitering not on conquer'd ground;
Looking forward, still pursuing,
    While the golden trumpets sound;
      King eternal!
    True to thee may we be found.

V.

Watching, hoping, toiling, praying,
  Till the victory is won,
May we then hear Jesus saying,
    "Toilers, rest! your work is done!"
      As we enter
    Homes of rest beyond the sun.

XI. . . . . S. M.

Come, my people, enter thou into thy chambers, and shut thy doors about thee.—Isa. xxvi. 20.

I.

ALONE with God to-day,
  My soul subdued and still,
My thoughts ascend the upward way
To Moses' lonely hill.

II.

From Nebo's utmost height
  Mine eyes look longingly
To the far distant land of light
  Beyond the glassy sea.

III.

I seem no stranger there,
  No traveller unknown:
For in that heavenly land so fair,
  My Lord is on the throne.

IV.

Among the company
Who serve Him day and night,
Dear ones who walk'd on earth with me
Walk now in robes of white.

V.

Their work and waiting done,
He call'd them of His grace;
Their higher service is begun
Before the Saviour's face.

VI.

I cannot know while here
The bliss of that sweet land;
But they have neither sin nor fear
Who in His presence stand.

VII.

So I in gladness wait
Before the Lord to-day,
While catching glimpses through the gate
Of glory far away.

1881.

XII. . . . . C. M.

𝔄 high priest...that hath been in all points tempted like as we are,
yet without sin.—Heb. vi. 15.

I.

WAS Jesus tempted like as we,
      The Holy One of God?
Were paths of pain and poverty
      By him, our Master, trod?

II.

Was there no place in all his earth
      To lay his head upon,
A King of more than royal birth,
      Yea, God's eternal Son?

III.

If thus the sinless Saviour fared,
      Can I, dare I repine,
When sorrow, want, and death he shared
      To make salvation mine!

IV.

O child redeem'd by his own blood,
  Why yield to anxious care?
Thou canst not sink beneath the flood
  When Christ is walking there.

V.

Think not thy Saviour does not see
  When Satan casts a dart:
No arrow ever wounded thee
  That did not pierce his heart.

VI.

The great High Priest is touch'd by all
  Thy weaknesses and woes;
And He, when grievous sorrows fall,
  Sufficient grace bestows.

1881.

XIII. . . . . S. M.

O Lord, my strength, and my fortress, and my refuge in the day of affliction.—Jer. xvi. 19.

I.

I HAVE no hiding-place,
  No refuge from the blast,
But in the arms of Jesus' grace
Around about me cast.

II.

Though I see not His hand,
  I feel its loving power:
And guardian angels near me stand
In my distressful hour.

III.

I dare not look within,
  But heavenward turn my gaze;
And lest my grief become my sin,
  My tongue breaks out in praise.

IV.

Though tears mine eyes bedim,
  He dries the tears I shed;
And in my soul I sing a hymn,
  Content and comforted.

1880.

XIV..... 8, 7, P.

𝔥im that turneth the shadow of death into the morning.
Amos v. 8.

I.

AFTER the darkness of the night
　Light cometh in the morning;
After the winter and its blight
　Spring wakes in new adorning.

II.

After the sowing of the seed
　The harvest greets the reaper;
After the day of loving deed
　Soft rest enfolds the sleeper.

III.

After the tempest's course is run
　A calm pervades the waters;
After the work of life is done
　God calls his sons and daughters.

IV.

After the closing of the eye
    They wake with Christ in heaven;
After the final victory
    The crown of life is given.

1981.

XV. . . . . C. M.

I.

THE morning of the centuries
  Beheld a light arise,
That in their heavenly ministries
  Ne'er fell on angels' eyes.

II.

Through all the ancient days it seem'd
  A planet new-begun;
It grew in fulness till it beam'd
  A sun beyond the sun.

III.

When earth with clouds of sin was dark,
  It made an open way;
E'en where it glimmer'd as a spark,
  Some souls received the ray;

IV.

And they became the sons of God
  Amid a scoffing race;
While bloody was the way they trod,
  His peace lit up their face.

V.

They seal'd their constancy with blood;
  And where the martyrs died
A multitude arose and stood,
  And God was glorified.

VI.

That sun has never ceased to shine
  Upon the King's domain,
Pouring from heaven a light divine
  To make its pathway plain.

VII.

Till centuries shall be no more,
  Its light shall not grow dim;
And Christ's redeem'd on heaven's shore
  Shall sing redemption's hymn.

1881.

4*

XVI. . . . . C. M.

Order my steps in thy word; and let not any iniquity have dominion over me.—Ps. cxix. 133.

I.

GIVE me to know thy will, O God,
And may I see to-day
A light from heaven upon my road
To clearly point the way:

II.

That I may know just what to do,
And what to leave undone,
And be unto thy service true
From dawn to setting sun:

III.

That I may speak the timely word,
And timely silence keep,—
By passion's hasty words unstirr'd
That cause the soul to weep:

IV.

That I may hold my thoughts in check,
 And every wild desire
That rises quick at pleasure's beck
 And flames into a fire:

V.

That I may kiss the needed rod,
 And patient bear the blow;
And say, 'Tis from the love of God;
 My Father wills it so.

VI.

Lord Jesus! from thy holy place
 The Spirit on me breathe:
Open the mantle of thy grace
 And keep my soul beneath.

1880.

XVII. . . . . 8, 7, 4.

But while he was yet afar off, his father saw him, and was moved with compassion.—Luke xv. 20.

I.

FAR away the Saviour saw me,
  Lost and wandering in the wild:
By his love he sought to draw me,—
Me unworthy and defiled,—
    As a father
Calls to him his erring child.

II.

I saw not the hand that beckon'd,
  I heard not his gracious call,
Till the joys on which I reckon'd,
  Worldly joys, had perish'd all;
    Then his mercy
Led me at his feet to fall.

III.

Jesus broke the chains that bound me,
    And his freeman I became:
Robes of grace he threw around me,
    Covering all my sin and shame:
        O how precious
    Is my great Deliverer's name!

IV.

Over all and bless'd forever,
    God on his eternal throne,
Who the bond of love can sever
    That unites to Christ his own?
        Lord Jehovah!
    Glory be to Thee alone.

1882.

XVIII. . . . . S. M.

O my God, my soul is cast down within me.—Ps. xlii. 6.

I.

M^Y soul cries out to God,
    Like children in the night,
Who fear some evil is abroad
    Because they see no light.

II.

There's darkness on the path,
    And pitfalls line the way,
Till fear of coming trouble hath
    An overpowering sway.

III.

It may be faith is weak;
    Perchance the heart is faint,
And in unutter'd words would speak
    Its longing, hungering plaint.

IV.

The duties left undone,
The follies unforgiven,
Rise up like clouds before the sun
And vail the face of heaven.

V.

So, desolate and lone,
The soul lifts up its cry
To Christ upon his gracious throne
Of majesty on high.

VI.

Lord, calm this restless mind,
From murmuring set me free,
And strength and comfort let me find
In earnest work for Thee.

1882.

XIX. . . . . C. M.

Therefore for thy name's sake lead me, and guide me.
Ps. xxxi. 3.

I.

LORD, take and lead me as a child
That knows not how to go,
Alike when day is calm and mild
And night's wild tempests blow.

II.

If grief and pain be mine to bear
And sorrows bow my head,
Let not my heart sink in despair
As though my Lord were dead.

III.

When I am weary, on the breast
Of Him who died for me
O let my laden spirit rest,
From care and worry free.

IV.

When joy shall fill my earth and skies
  With a serenest calm,
Then may my thoughts to Thee arise
  In one continual psalm.

V.

When some sad brother turns to me
  In sore and heavy grief,
May I be quick in sympathy
  And quicker in relief.

VI

When some poor soul is sick of sin
  And seeks the way to God,
O make me wise that soul to win
  To take the heavenward road.

VII.

Lord, in the dark and in the light
  Still keep me in thy way,
A child whose hand is claspéd tight
  In thine by night and day.

1875.

XX. . . . . C. M.

Even there shall thy hand lead me, and thy right hand shall hold me.
Ps. cxxxix. 10.

I.

AGAIN I take with hopeful heart
    My life's allotted task :
To do it well the grace impart ;
    This, Lord, I humbly ask.

II.

The day's perplexing mysteries
    I may not understand :
Be it enough my Father sees
    And holds them in his hand.

III.

My duty for the day is plain,—
    To go where God shall call,
Or, patient, hold the tangled skein
    While he unravels all.

IV.

I may not ask that no rough wind
    Upon my head shall blow,
Yet I may pray that I shall find
    Strength in the day of wo.

V.

The sun may shine through all the day,
    Or clouds may hide the sky,
But while God's love lights up my way
    I know his hand is nigh.

1882.

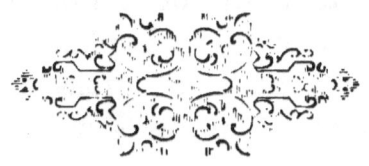

XXI. . . . . C. M.

Canst thou by searching find out God? canst thou find out the
Almighty unto perfection.—Job xi. 7.

I.

IN vain the ways of Providence
   With anxious gaze I scan:
To find out God by human sense
   It is not given to man.

II.

Enough to know he cannot err
   When worlds his plans fulfil;
That not a blade of grass can stir
   But at its Maker's will.

III.

Enough to know that God is just,
   Yet with a father's heart;
Enough with loving faith to trust
   When earthly friends depart.

IV.

Enough to know he gave his Son
   My guilt and grief to bear,
That I, though by my sin undone,
   Might still his mercy share.

V.

Then let me nevermore repine
   Beneath the chastening stroke,
And be the willing spirit mine
   To wear the Saviour's yoke.

18P..

XXII. . . . . C. M.

Take thy part in suffering hardship, as a good soldier of Christ Jesus.—2 Tim. ii. 3.

I.

WHILE some may run an easy pace
With self-reliant boast,
The Lord e'er gives to those his grace
Who seek and need it most.

II.

Beneath a quiet smile may lie
A sorrow of the soul
That needs a daily victory
To hold it in control.

III.

And they who bear the battle's brunt,
And temper'd weapons wield,
Shall stand up grandly in the front
And hold the conquer'd field.

IV.

God's rank and file, in battle line
    And truth's divine array,
Shall set their camp at day's decline
    Along the King's highway

V.

To that good land, by sense unknown,—
    That land whose name is Heaven,—
Where Christ doth gather all his own,
    And crowns of life are given.

1881.

XXIII..... 8, 7, 4.

𝔒ur 𝔏orð 𝔍ɛsus 𝔠ɦrist ... tɦɛ ƀlɛssɛð anð onlɒ 𝔓otɛntatɛ, tɦɛ 𝔎ing
of kings, anð 𝔏orð of lorðs; ɱɦo onlɒ ɦatɦ immortalitɒ, ðɱɛlling in
light unapproaɛɦaƀlɛ, ɱɦom no man ɦatɦ sɛɛn, nor ɛan sɛɛ:
to ɱɦom ƀɛ ɦonour anð poɱɛr ɛtɛrnal. 𝔄mɛn.
1 Tim. vi. 14-16.

I.

BLESSED be thy name forever,
    Lord and Christ, eternal King!
While we live, our tongues shall never
    Fail thy glorious praise to sing,—
        While before Thee
    Thankful offerings we bring.

II.

In the fulness of the ages
    Thou as man didst come to earth:
Welcomed by the wisest sages,
    Israel saw not thy worth,—
        Yet what glory
    Heralded thy wondrous birth!

III.

Scorn'd by cruel men, they slew thee,
    Thou the Maker of them all!
Though so few were they that knew thee,
    Blest were they whom thou didst call,—
        Like their Master,
    By the hand of man to fall.

IV.

Throned in thy eternal glory,
    Myriads worship at thy feet:
May we bend with them before thee
    When our work shall be complete,—
        By thy Spirit
    Made for heavenly service meet.

1882.

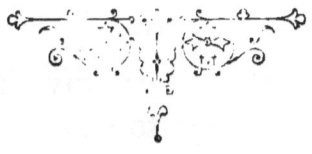

XXIV. . . . . 8, 7.

Come unto me, all ye that labour and are heavy laden, and I will
give you rest.—Matt. xi. 28.

I.

A T the door of mercy sighing
⠀⠀With the burden of my sin,
Day and night my soul is crying,
⠀⠀"Open, Lord, and let me in."
Waiting mid the darkness dreary,
⠀⠀⠀⠀Stretching out my hands to Thee,
In the refuge for the weary
⠀⠀⠀⠀Is there not a place for me?

II.

I have sought to earn thy favour,
⠀⠀⠀⠀Caring not for toil or cost;
Yet I find not him my Saviour,
⠀⠀⠀⠀Him who came to seek the lost.
Blessed Master! in thy pity
⠀⠀⠀⠀Teach me what I ought to do,
So that in the holy city
⠀⠀⠀⠀I may gain an entrance too.

III.

Hark! what sounds mine ear receiveth,
   Sweet as songs of seraphim!
"He that in the Lord believeth
   Life eternal hath in Him.
At the outer door why staying?
   Nothing, soul! hast thou to pay:
Christ in love to thee is saying,
   Weary child, come in to-day."

IV.

I knew not of Jesus' kindness!
   I knew not of Jesus' grace!
O the blackness of the blindness
   That could not behold his face!
I saw not the door was open,
   Nor my Lord invite me in:
Grace is mine beyond my hoping,
   Mercy mightier than my sin.

1871.

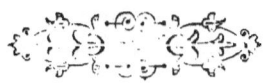

XXV. . . . . 8, 7, 4.

Fear not; I am the first and the last. . . . I am the Alpha and the
Omega, the beginning and the end. I will give unto him that is
athirst of the fountain of the water of life freely.
Rev. i. 17. xxi. 6.

I.

JESUS! when my soul is parting
From this body frail and weak,
And the deathly dew is starting
Down this pale and wasted cheek,—
Thine, my Saviour,
Be the name I last shall speak.

II.

Jesus! when my memory wanders
Far from loved ones at my side,
And in fitful dreaming ponders
Who are they that near me glide,—
Last, my Saviour,
Let my thoughts on thee abide.

III.

When the morn in all its glory
   Charms no more mine ear nor eye,
And the shadows closing o'er me
   Warn me of the time to die,—
     Last, my Saviour,
   Let me see thee standing by.

IV.

When my feet shall pass the river,
   And upon the farther shore
I shall walk, redeem'd for ever,
   Ne'er to sin—to die no more,—
     First, Lord Jesus!
   Let me see thee, and adore.

1843.

XXVI. . . . . C. M.

The peace of God, which passeth all understanding.—Phil. iv. 7.

I.

MY soul is resting in God's peace,
Without a care or fear:
The tumults of my bosom cease,
For Christ my Lord is here.

II.

The Spirit poureth from on high
A sanctifying tide;
And, bathing in its stream of joy,
My soul is satisfied.

III.

He driveth curious doubts away,
He giveth childlike faith;
And so I take the yea or nay
Just as my Saviour saith.

IV.

I have not other wish to be
    Than what my Lord ordains;
So what He knoweth best for me,
    That be my richest gains.

V.

A spirit meek and quieted
    Is better than a crown;
How rich the blessing on the head
    That Jesus sendeth down!

VI.

Here in his banquet-house I bide,
    His banner o'er me love,
And wait the coming eventide
    Of perfect peace above.

1870.

XXVII. . . . . 6, 5.

𝔇𝔯𝔞𝔴 𝔫𝔦𝔤𝔥 𝔱𝔬 𝔊𝔬𝔡, 𝔞𝔫𝔡 𝔥𝔢 𝔴𝔦𝔩𝔩 𝔡𝔯𝔞𝔴 𝔫𝔦𝔤𝔥 𝔱𝔬 𝔶𝔬𝔲.—James iv. 8.

I.

DRAW nigh to the Holy,
  Bend low at His throne;
There, penitent, lowly,
  Thy sinfulness own:
There, there, if thou yearnest
  For pardon and rest,
There, fervent and earnest,
  Prefer thy request.

II.

Confess thy backsliding,
  Thy weakness and fears;
In Jesus confiding,
  There pour out thy tears.
Think not He will scorn thee,
  Though wretched thy case;
His hands will adorn thee
  With garments of grace.

III.

More precious than treasure,
　More vast than the sea,
His love has no measure
　Nor limit to thee.
His easy yoke wearing,
　His pleasure abide;
In all thy cross-bearing,
　He'll walk by thy side.

IV.

Fear not the wild clangour
　That Satan may raise,
So God's righteous anger
　But pass from thy ways.
Whom Christ has forgiven
　Goes safely along,
Till in the high heaven
　He sings the new song.

V.

Then kneel to the Holy,
　Bend low at His throne;
There, penitent lowly,
　Thy sinfulness own:
There, soul! if thou yearnest
　For pardon and rest,
There, fervent and earnest,
　Prefer thy request. 1852.

XXVIII. . . . . 7's.

𝔕𝔢𝔪𝔢𝔪𝔟𝔢𝔯 𝔱𝔥𝔢 sabbath ban, to keep it holy.—Ex. xx. 8.
And on the sabbath they rested according to the commandment.
Luke xxiii. 56.

I.

H ALLOW'D day of sacred rest,
   Welcome, welcome to my breast:
All the week I've sigh'd to feel
Bliss thine hours alone reveal.

II.

Aching temples, throb no more;
Busy care, thy reign is o'er;
Troublous thoughts, flee far away
From this quiet resting-day.

III.

Faith's anticipations, rise!
Leap the barriers to the skies:
Upward soar, my soul, to Him
Loved by saints and seraphim.

IV.

Thankful praise, my lips, employ—
Utter all my rapturous joy:
Though o'er all things silence come,
Can a ransom'd soul be dumb?

V.

Priceless moments! rich and sweet:
Happy soul! at Jesus' feet,
Rest, oh rest!—when He is near,
Lovingly, hast thou a fear?

VI.

Master! lowly here I lie:
Look on me with gracious eye;
Lay the yoke of love on me,
Easy shall the burden be!

VII.

Saviour! may thy Sabbaths come
Laden with the hope of home:
On the day thy grace has given,
Fit me for thyself and heaven.

1842.

XXIX. . . . . C. M.

What time I am afraid, I will trust in thee.—Ps. lvi. 3.

I.

THE billows round me rise and roll,
　　The storms of worldly care
Beat heavily upon my soul,
　　And shroud me in despair:
Forsaken, comfortless, betray'd,
　　With none to succour me,—
Father! what time I am afraid,
　　Then will I trust in Thee!

II.

As feeble as the bruisèd reed,
　　Infirm to will or do;
Oft working out the ungrateful deed
　　'Twere better to eschew;
How were the sinking soul dismay'd
　　But for this refuge-plea,—
Father, what time I am afraid,
　　Then will I trust in Thee!

III.

When hope is faint, and faith is weak,
    And fears the bosom fill,
And I a strong assurance seek
    That thou art gracious still;
I rest upon thy promise-word,
    To thine own truth I flee:
Father, what time I am afraid,
    Then will I trust in Thee!

IV.

When saintly paleness marks my face,
    And dimness fills mine eye,
And, hoping only in thy grace,
    I bow my head to die;
If, entering in the vale of shade,
    Nor sun nor star I see,
Father, what time I am afraid,
    Then will I trust in Thee!

1853.

XXX. . . . . C. M.

𝔚𝔢 𝔭𝔯𝔞𝔶𝔢𝔡 𝔞𝔤𝔞𝔦𝔫; 𝔞𝔫𝔡 𝔱𝔥𝔢 𝔥𝔢𝔞𝔳𝔢𝔫 𝔤𝔞𝔳𝔢 𝔯𝔞𝔦𝔫, 𝔞𝔫𝔡 𝔱𝔥𝔢 𝔢𝔞𝔯𝔱𝔥 𝔟𝔯𝔬𝔲𝔤𝔥𝔱 𝔣𝔬𝔯𝔱𝔥 𝔥𝔢𝔯 𝔣𝔯𝔲𝔦𝔱.—James v. 18.

I.

O GRACIOUS Father! send us showers,
The gentle showers of rain,
To cheer the corn, the grass, the flowers,
On mountain-side and plain.

II.

Command the pregnant clouds to rise
And vail the fiery sun,
While from the fountains of the skies
The streams of blessing run.

III.

O gracious Father! send us showers;
The cattle mutely stand
Amid the scorch'd and wither'd bowers;
Have mercy on our land!

IV.

The spider's web is on the mead,
    The worm consumes the leaf;
And all thy works before Thee plead
    The silent plea of grief.

V.

O gracious Father! send us showers;
    Regard our earnest cries;
But meek submission still be ours
    While our petitions rise.

VI.

To Thee each living thing looks up;
    Thou mad'st—thou'lt not destroy:
The overflow of mercy's cup
    Shall wake creation's joy.

1852.

XXXI. . . . . L. M.

𝔉𝔬𝔯 𝔰𝔬 𝔥𝔢 𝔤𝔦𝔟𝔢𝔱𝔥 𝔥𝔦𝔰 𝔟𝔢𝔩𝔬𝔟𝔢𝔡 𝔰𝔩𝔢𝔢𝔭.—Ps. cxxvii. 2.

I.

IN tearless anguish once I lay,
  And every tender string of life
Was rudely smitten by disease,
  And nature quiver'd in the strife.

II.

To God I look'd for help the while
  The lingering moments seem'd to creep,
These words of grace broke on my mind,
  "He giveth his belovèd sleep."

III.

A gentle peace, like evening winds
  In summer from the ocean's breast,
Moved o'er my sighing, sinking soul,
  And soothed my murmurings all to rest;

IV.

And through that weary night of pain,
　　When it were manliness to weep,
My soul was comforted by this,
　　"He giveth his belovèd sleep."

V.

When prison'd long, my soul would fain
　　Leap through her fragile walls and flee,
But on the unmeasured life beyond
　　She, halting, gazes tremblingly;

VI.

Then may I simply trust in Him
　　Whose arms his feeblest follower keep,
And close mine eyes, and say, in death,
　　"He giveth his belovèd sleep!"

1842.

XXXII. . . . . C. M.

Or ever the silver cord be loosed, or the golden bowl be broken.
Eccl. xii. 6.

I.

THE day is wearing fast away,
    The night is coming on,
To end the earthly pilgrimage
    Begun at being's dawn.

II.

The voice of earthly friends no more
    Within my soul can reach ;
Another world hath round me grown,
    Earth hath another speech.

III.

Now fain am I to go when He
    Who sent me here shall call :
I wait his gentle breath to cause
    The ancient tree to fall.

IV.

I long to lay my burden down,
    And in earth's bosom rest
As calmly as an infant sleeps
    Upon its mother's breast.

V.

Welcome, approaching shades of even,
    By idling triflers shunn'd!
I see the immortal life of heaven,
    And Christ, my God, beyond!

1840.

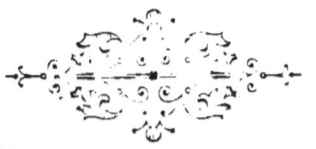

XXXIII. . . . .8, 7, 4.

Peter was grieved because he said unto him the third time, Lovest thou me? And he said unto him, Lord, thou knowest all things; thou knowest that I love thee.—John xxi. 17.

I.

ART thou in thy spirit lowly,
   Like the Man of Nazareth?
Art thou seeking to be wholly
   Join'd to him, come life, come death?
      Lov'st thou Jesus
   More than thine own vital breath?

II.

Is thy bosom full of sorrow?
   Is a cloud upon thy way?
Why the worldling's burden borrow?
   Child of grace and promise, say!
      Lov'st thou Jesus?
   Joy should be thy guest to-day.

III.

Hath God made all men to praise thee?
Or art thou to fame unknown?
Only seek that he should raise thee
Up to an immortal throne.
Lov'st thou Jesus?
He'll provide for all his own.

IV.

Care not thou how low thy station,
If thy God hath chosen thee
Heir of glory and salvation
Now and evermore to be!
Lov'st thou Jesus?
Life is thine eternally.

1870.

XXXIV. . . . . C. M.

Then he arose, and rebuked the winds and the sea; and there was a great calm.—Matt. viii. 26.

I.

THE darkness of the night came down
  And on my soul it lay,
As if my righteous Maker's frown
  Were gathering round my way.

II.

As lonely as if I alone
  In all the earth were left,—
As helpless as an infant-one
  Of mother's care bereft,—

III.

How swift and sure had been my doom
  Had Christ forgotten me!
A voice arose amid the gloom,
  "Thy Saviour loveth thee!"

IV.

Immediately there was a calm,
A calm without, within;
For Jesus wrote upon my palm
Full pardon of my sin.

V.

The inward tempests rage no more,
The spirit's sorrows cease,
When Jesus stands upon the shore,
And gently whispers, "Peace!"

1846.

XXXV. . . . . 8, 7, 4.

𝔈 shall give thee the heathen for thine inheritance, and the uttermost parts of the earth for thy possession.—Ps. ii. 8.

I.

GOD has said it,—and his promise
   Stands as firmly as his throne,—
Earth shall be a sure possession
   Granted to his Son alone;
     And the heathen
Jesus' gracious reign shall own.

II.

Where a soul in guilt is lying,
   There his gospel shall be sent;
Life and grace for wretches dying,
   Balm for bosoms sad and rent:
     News of mercy,
All shall hear the call, Repent!

III.

Thou the Lord of all creation,
    Every living soul is thine:
May the grace of thy salvation
    On the lands of darkness shine:
        Holy Spirit!
    To thyself the world incline.

IV.

Words of precious promise, spoken
    In thy faithfulness and love,
Never, never can be broken
    While thou reignest King above:
        Let thy mercies
    Thy abounding goodness prove.

1841.

XXXVI. . . . . 7, 6.

Yea, though I walk through the valley of the shadow of death, I will
fear no evil: for thou art with me; thy rod and thy staff
they comfort me.—Ps. xxiii. 4.

I.

THERE is a land immortal,
    The beautiful of lands;
Beside its ancient portal
    A sentry grimly stands:
He only can undo it,
    And open wide the door;
And mortals who pass through it
    Are mortal nevermore.

II.

That glorious land is Heaven,
    And Death the sentry grim:
The Lord thereof has given
    The opening keys to him;
And ransom'd spirits, sighing
    And sorrowful for sin,
Pass through the gate in dying,
    And freely enter in.

III.

Though dark and drear the passage
    That leads unto the gate,
Yet grace attends the message
    To souls that watch and wait;
And at the time appointed
    A messenger comes down,
And guides the Lord's anointed
    From cross to glory's crown.

IV.

Their sighs are lost in singing;
    They're blessed in their tears:
Their journey heavenward winging,
    They leave on earth their fears.
Death like an angel seeming,
    "We welcome thee!" they cry:
Their eyes with glory gleaming,
    'Tis life for them to die.

1845.

XXXVII. . . . . L. M.

It is God which worketh in you both to will and to work, for his good pleasure.—Phil. ii. 13.

I.

'TIS well that thou, my God, shouldst be
    The master of my destiny;
For were my lot placed in my hand,
Where should my sure salvation stand?

II.

Beset around with wily snares,
And cumber'd with uncounted cares,
What arm but thine alone can hold
My soul within thy saving fold?

III.

The things of sense allure mine eyes,
And sudden sins my soul surprise:
Were I no more thy grace to share,
Then naught were left me but despair.

IV.

I know that I am safe with thee;
Then in thy hands my portion be:
I cannot fear what may betide
When on thyself my hopes abide.

V.

Let sinless ones on merit stand,
I seek for mercy at thy hand:
No other way of help I see,
Thy grace in Christ must work for me.

VI.

A wretch were I to lean upon
The works my erring hands have done:
I stand a suppliant, with the plea,
Atoning blood was shed for me.

VII.

O let thy Spirit day by day
Uphold me in the upward way:
Enough for me that thou wilt keep
The feeblest of thy chosen sheep.

XXXVIII. . . . . 8, 7.

Let not your heart be troubled: ye believe in God, believe also in me.
John xiv. 1.

I.

BEAR the burden of the present,
  Let the morrow bear its own;
If the morning sky be pleasant,
  Why the coming night bemoan?

II.

If the darken'd heavens lower,
  Wrap thy cloak around thy form;
Though the tempest rise in power,
  God is mightier than the storm.

III.

Steadfast faith and hope unshaken
  Animate the trusting breast;
Step by step the journey's taken
  Nearer to the land of rest.

IV.

All unseen, the Master walketh
  By the toiling servant's side:
Comfortable words he talketh,
  While his hands uphold and guide.

V.

Grief, nor pain, nor any sorrow
  Rends thy breast to him unknown;
He to-day and He to-morrow
  Grace sufficient gives his own.

VI.

Holy strivings nerve and strengthen,
  Long endurance wins the crown:
When the evening shadows lengthen,
  Thou shalt lay the burden down.

1852.

XXXIX. . . . . C. M.

A host compassed the city both with horses and chariots.
2 Kings vi. 15.

I.

UNSEEN by them, a glorious host
About God's people stand:
The heavenly watchers hold the post
At his supreme command.

II.

There is no child of God too high
To need their constant care,
And none too deep in poverty
Their daily help to share.

III.

When loved ones go, and earth is lone,
As if no friend were near,
Then unseen angels from the throne
Bring helpful words of cheer.

IV.

The sun of hope breaks through our gloom,
    And wondering whence it came,
We start, like Mary at the tomb
    When Jesus call'd her name.

V.

Say, who can snatch from God away
    His blood-redeeméd ones?
And who the heavenward course can stay
    Of God Almighty's sons?

1882.

8*

XL. . . . . C. M.

The ransomed of the Lord...shall come to Zion with songs.
Isa. xxxv. 10.

I.

FAR distant from my Father's house
　　I would no longer stay;
But gird my soul and hasten on,
　　And sing upon the way!

II.

The skies are dark, the thunders roll,
　　And lightnings round me play;
Let me but feel my Saviour near,
　　I'll sing upon the way!

III.

The night is long and drear, I cry;
　　O when will come the day?
I see the morning-star arise,
　　And sing upon the way!

IV.

When care and sickness bow my frame,
    And all my powers decay,
I'll ask Him for His promised grace,
    And sing upon the way!

V.

He'll not forsake me when I'm old,
    And weak, and blind, and gray;
I'll lean upon his faithfulness,
    And sing upon the way!

VI.

When angels bear me home to heaven,
    Disrobed of mortal clay,
I'll enter in the pearly gates,
    And sing upon the way!

1842.

XLI......8, 7, P.

The Lord is good to all; and his tender mercies are over all his works.—Ps. cxlv. 9.

I.

OVER the earth a stillness comes,
  The eventide is falling:
Lord, bless all dwellers in their homes
  Who on thy name are calling.

II.

Thy blessing on the toiler rest;
  The over-worn and weary;
The dying, and the comfortless
  To whom the earth is dreary.

III.

Thy blessing on the child to-night;
  Thy blessing on the hoary;
The maiden clad in beauty bright,
  The young man in his glory.

IV.

Thy blessing on my fellow-race,
  Of every clime and nation:
May they partake thy saving grace,
  O Giver of salvation.

V.

If any man have wrought me wrong,
  Still blessings be upon him:
May I in love to him be strong,
  Till charity have won him.

VI.

Thy blessings on me, from of old,
  My God! I cannot number:
I wrap me in their ample fold,
  And sink in trustful slumber.

1853.

XLII. . . . . L. M.

Take a psalm, and bring hither the timbrel, the pleasant harp with the psaltery.—Ps. lxxxi. 2.

I.

LET all the people sing a psalm,
    A stately psalm of solemn praise,
While sitting in the holy calm,
    The calm befitting Sabbath days.

II.

Come, chant the words King David sang
    When heavenly airs around him swept,
And Zion's tents with music rang,
    While holy day the singers kept.

III.

The King of glory on his throne,
    The Ancient of eternal days,
The infinite and triune One,
    Immortal strains become his praise.

IV.

Let all the tribes of Adam's race,
   With thankful voice and lifted palms,
E'er magnify his truth and grace
   And laud him in the ancient psalms.

1868.

XLIII. .... C. M.

𝔈𝔣 𝔞𝔫𝔤 𝔪𝔞𝔫 𝔱𝔥𝔦𝔯𝔰𝔱, 𝔩𝔢𝔱 𝔥𝔦𝔪 𝔠𝔬𝔪𝔢 𝔲𝔫𝔱𝔬 𝔪𝔢, 𝔞𝔫𝔡 𝔡𝔯𝔦𝔫𝔨.—John vii. 37.

I.

I LONG for God, the living God;
  I hunger for his grace :
I long to see as I have seen
  My heavenly Saviour's face.

II.

The earth has not a home for me
  Where I would always stay :
O let me take my pilgrim-staff
  And speed my upward way.

III.

I would not be afraid to live,
  Nor yet afraid to die ;
Nor wish to end my working days,
  Or make them faster fly.

IV.

But I would hide myself beneath
    Jehovah's sheltering wing,
And wait till his appointed hour
    Shall life immortal bring.

V.

Lord, may I learn to work or wait,
    Just as thy word is given,—
Not loitering idly at the gate
    That opens into heaven.

1866.

XLIV. . . . . 8, 7.

Whom the Lord loveth he chasteneth, and scourgeth every son whom he receiveth.—Heb. xii. 6.

I.

WHEN he waketh, when he sleepeth,
　　When he toileth in the day,
Him the Father safely keepeth
　　Who makes Christ his only stay.

II.

If he wanders, God will chasten
　　Him with many stripes or few,
Till his erring footsteps hasten
　　To the mercy-seat anew.

III.

If he meekly beareth crosses,
　　And his eyes yet look to heaven,
God will turn to gain his losses,
　　Yea, to him will much be given.

IV.

Daily he will find a token
    That his Lord loves to the end :
When the golden bowl is broken,
    Up to him shall he ascend.

V.

No more sin and no more sorrow,
    No more bitter tears to shed ;
Heaven will have no sad to-morrow,
    But eternal day instead.

1882.

XLV. . . . . S. M.

𝔗𝔥𝔢 𝔏𝔬𝔯𝔡 𝔴𝔦𝔩𝔩 𝔰𝔱𝔯𝔢𝔫𝔤𝔱𝔥𝔢𝔫 𝔥𝔦𝔪 𝔲𝔭𝔬𝔫 𝔱𝔥𝔢 𝔟𝔢𝔡 𝔬𝔣 𝔩𝔞𝔫𝔤𝔲𝔦𝔰𝔥𝔦𝔫𝔤.
Ps. xli. 3.

I.

A PRISONER of the Lord,
   Awaiting his commands,
My prison-house is amply stored
With bounties from his hands.

II.

He makes my pillow soft
   While prostrate, weak, and sore,
And ministering angels oft
   Enter my chamber-door.

III.

Sweet love in every tone
   Is whisper'd round my bed:
I know that none will give a stone
   Instead of strengthening bread.

IV.

No fears my soul alarm;
My pains shall pass away:
Christ puts his everlasting arm
Beneath me all the day.

V.

How can I be cast down?
Why wrap myself in gloom,
And wear a care-begotten frown,
When Christ is in the room?

VI.

God's strokes are not in wrath:
The fruits that feed the soul
Bestrew the strait and narrow path
Unto the heavenly goal.

1882.

XLVI. . . . . L. M.

Secretly saying, The Master is here, and calleth thee.—John xi. 28.

I.

SOME day the word will come to me,
Arise; the Master calls for thee.
May I be ready then to go,
Saying, Lord Jesus! even so.

II.

Will work I've purposed in my thought
Be to my Master's pleasure wrought?
And will more talents then be won,
So that the Lord may say, Well done?

III.

Will tears be shed upon my bier
By some I've help'd to comfort here?
Will seed I've sown some fruitage bear
Too late for me the joy to share?

IV.

Shall I on Jordan's farther side
Find some redeem'd and glorified
To whom I pointed out the road
Leading to that divine abode?

V.

I cannot answer Yea or Nay:
This only, Master, can I say:
If I've done aught to honour thee,
It was thy grace that wrought through me.

VI.

O blessed Lord, in me abide
When I pass over Jordan's tide,
That I with my last trembling breath
May glorify thy name in death.

1882.

XLVII. . . . . C. M.

𝔒n that day, the first day of the week, . . . Jesus came and stood
in the midst.—John xx. 19.

I.

THE blessing of the Sabbath-day
   Again our spirit cheers,
And heaven seems not so far away
   That on our listening ears

II.

Some sounds of music may not fall
   Struck on angelic lyres,
Some anthems to the Lord, by all
   The high celestial choirs.

III.

Let our lips, too, break forth in praise
   To thee, O King of heaven,
For this the chiefest of the days,
   The holiest of the seven.

IV.

O Thou who on this day didst rise
  Omnipotent above,
Reveal to our expectant eyes
  New glimpses of thy love.

V.

Come, Holy Comforter, and show
  Thy gracious sovereign power,
That we may more like Jesus grow
  In this accepted hour.

VI.

As on the day of Pentecost,
  Visit thy church again,
That earth may join the heavenly host
  In praising Thee. Amen.

1882.

XLVIII. . . . . C. M.

Things which eye saw not, and ear heard not, and which entered not into the heart of man.—1 Cor. ii. 9.

I.

NO tongue of man has ever told
    God's everlasting love;
No heart has known the manifold
    Delights prepared above.

II.

Eye has not seen, ear has not heard
    These great and marvellous things,
Laid up for all who trust his word,
    For poor as well as kings.

III.

God's children daily something learn
    While training in his schools:
More clearly do their minds discern
    How gracious are his rules:

IV.

Yet little can they apprehend
    What God has still in store;
For that which has no bound nor end
    They cannot reckon o'er.

V.

Glory to thee, eternal King!
    Invisible, yet known
To loving souls who daily bring
    Faith's offering to thy throne.

1842.

XLIX. . . . . C. M.

𝔍𝔢𝔰𝔲𝔰 𝔰𝔞𝔦𝔡 𝔱𝔥𝔢𝔯𝔢𝔣𝔬𝔯𝔢 𝔲𝔫𝔱𝔬 𝔱𝔥𝔢 𝔱𝔴𝔢𝔩𝔟𝔢, 𝔚𝔬𝔲𝔩𝔡 𝔶𝔢 𝔞𝔩𝔰𝔬 𝔤𝔬 𝔞𝔴𝔞𝔶?
John vi. 67.

I.

WHERE could I go but unto thee,
O man of Nazareth?
Thy blood was shed on Calvary
To give me life for death!

II.

To whom, my Lord, but unto thee,
  O Son of God most high,
When angels bend with reverent knee
Before thy majesty?

III.

Where can I go but unto thee,
The only refuge-tower
Impregnable, where I can flee
In sore temptation's hour?

IV.

To whom need I go but to thee?
  Thou art the utmost sum
Of every soul's necessity;—
  And therefore, Lord, I come.

V.

O Lamb of God, who cam'st to take
  The sin of man away,
Fast hold me for thy mercy's sake,
  And I shall never stray.

1882.

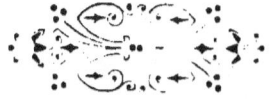

L. . . . C. M.

*For as often as ye eat this bread, and drink the cup, ye proclaim
the Lord's death till he come.—1 Cor. xi. 26.*

I.

AS children dwelling in their home
By right of grace divine,
Unto thy table, Lord, we come
To take of bread and wine.

II.

The bread shows forth thy body slain,
The wine thy blood out-pour'd:
To take away our sin and stain
Cost thy dear life, O Lord.

III.

O may the Holy Ghost descend
With blessing from above,
That grateful praise may now ascend
For thine amazing love.

IV.

Abide with us this holy day
And fill us with thy peace,
And while we gladly praise and pray,
Lord, make our faith increase.

V.

Sit with us at the blessed feast,
As in the day of old,
Our high and sovereign Saviour-Priest,
Thy glory to behold.

1882.

LI. . . . . 7's.

There was at the table reclining in Jesus' bosom one of his disciples, whom Jesus loved.—John xiii. 23.

I.

IN the hidden ways of life
    God's belovéd may be found,
Shut in from the things of strife,
    Hedged with mercies all around.

II.

Born of God they know not when,
    Single is the faith they hold,
Prying not with curious ken
    Into what has not been told.

III.

Like the saint of Patmos isle,
    In them love has potent sway,
Israelites who have no guile,
    Passing on their heavenward way:

IV.

By the loving, kindly deed,
 By the strengthening word of cheer,
By the helpful hand in need,
 Glorifying Jesus here.

V.

Pointing out the path to heaven,
 Winning souls is their reward:
When the welcome-call is given,
 Dying, they wake in the Lord.

1882.

LII. . . . . 7's.

After ye were enlightened, ye endured a great conflict of sufferings.
Heb. x. 32.

I.

IN the midnight and the storm
    Some of God's beloved must go;
Not for them the valleys warm,
    But the hills of crag and snow.

II.

In the darkness call'd to stand,
    Fighting with a foe unseen,
Friend nor lover at their hand,
    Strongly on their Lord they lean.

III.

Chasten'd sore, bereaved, and lone,
    They with steadfast faith look up,
Seeking, low before his throne,
    Grace to take the bitter cup.

IV.

Not the less beloved are they,
  Heirs with Christ, who suffer loss:
They shall find, some coming day,
  Why 'twas theirs to bear the cross.

V.

Some the fight of faith must share;
  Some endure the tempter's blows;
Testimony they must bear
  Christ is mightier than his foes.

VI.

As they lay their weapons by,
  Conquerors in the final strife,
Glory be to God! they cry,
  Entering into restful life.

1882.

LIII. . . . . C. M.

Jesus answered him, If I wash thee not, thou hast no part with me.
John xiii. 8.

I.

THE dusty paths of earth defile
My sandals through the day;
And vexing cares my soul beguile
While toiling on the way.

II.

How oft I lose the gracious sense
Of nearness unto Thee!
How oft forget the providence
That orders life for me!

III.

The daily good that I would do
Is often unbegun;
And evil I would fain eschew
My heedless hands have done.

IV.

At eventime, unsatisfied,
    I call the day to mind;
And by thy righteous standard tried,
    Shortcomings do I find.

V.

O Thou who, in thy graciousness,
    Didst wash thy servants' feet,
Thy travel-stain'd disciple bless
    Before thy mercy-seat.

VI.

The robe of works that I have worn
    Is scanty for my needs:
Give me the robe of thy new-born,—
    Of faith and holy deeds.

1882.

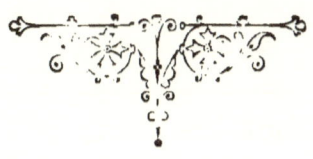

LIV. . . . . S. M.

Ye are not your own; for ye were bought with a price.
1 Cor. vi. 19, 20.

I.

I GIVE myself to God,
My life, my soul, my all:
He knows the devious paths I've trod,
In mercy's hand I fall.

II.

My sins I cannot count,
Nor sum his favours up:
I humbly kneel at mercy's fount
And take salvation's cup.

III.

I proffer but his own;
And may the Master take
The gift I lay before his throne,
For my Redeemer's sake.

IV.

I give myself to God,
  For evermore to hold:
I pass beneath the Shepherd's rod
  To bide within his fold.

1882.

LV. . . . .C. M.

And him that cometh to me I will in no wise cast out.—John vi. 37.

I.

THE pathway to the mercy-seat
   Is found of all who will;
And they who kneel at Jesus' feet
   Find him a Saviour still.

II.

As, when upon the earth he trod,
   None empty went away
Who sought his blessing as their God,
   So we to him may pray.

III.

The child unto his parent runs
   For comfort and relief:
So may the Lord's redeeméd ones
   Go to him with their grief.

IV.

Yea, even in the busiest hour
    Unspoken prayer may rise,
And blessings in a gracious shower
    Fall on us from the skies.

V.

We bless and magnify thy name,
    O Thou that answerest prayer:
In every age thou art the same
    To all who trust thy care.

1882.

LVI. . . . . C. M.

As many as touched him were made whole.—Mark vi. 56.

I.

AT Jesus' feet I take my place:
    I touch his garment's hem:
A helpless child in need of grace
    My Lord will not condemn.

II.

I have no hope but in his love;
    His promise is my plea:
I give myself to Him who strove
    E'en unto death for me.

III.

I only ask that I may know
    What he would have me do,
That my obedient life may show
    The grace that bears me through.

IV.

I've nothing, Lord, to offer thee
But this weak heart of mine:
O take it, Lord, and let it be
Thine own, for ever thine.

1882.

LVII. . . . . C. M.

And the rock was Christ.—1 Cor. x. 4.

I.

GIVE me a foothold on the rock:
  The billows round me roll:
Let not their wild, impetuous shock
  O'erwhelm my trembling soul.
O Thou that walkest on the wave,
  Thou Ruler of the sea,
Stretch forth thy mighty arm to save
  The soul that calls on thee.

II.

Give me a foothold on the rock,
  O Saviour of the lost!
The world and sin my struggles mock,
  And I am tempest-tost.
I strive to reach an anchoring place:
  My God, give me a stay;
Extend to me thy hand of grace,
  Lest I be cast away.

III.

Give me a foothold on the rock,
    Till voices 'yond the sea,
Like evening chimings of the clock,
    Bid welcome home to me.
The day of toil and watching o'er,
    The night of sorrow past,
I step upon the eternal shore,
    And rest in peace at last.

1882.

LVIII. . . . . 7's.

The Lord lift up his countenance upon thee, and give thee peace.
Num. vi. 26.

I.

REST and peace for Jesus' sake!
    O my Father, hear my cry;
Heal my bosom's bitter ache,
    While before thy feet I lie.

II.

I have loved and I have lost
    Those whom I had prized too well:
O'er my threshold sorrow cross'd
    When the cherish'd idols fell.

III.

I forgot that they were lent,
    And I claim'd them as my own,
Till the message from thee sent
    Took them up before thy throne.

IV.

Speak the word of peace to me;
  Pardon thy forgetful child:
Let me find my rest in thee,
  Comforted and reconciled:

V.

Comforted, that loving eyes
  Shone so long within my home:
Reconciled, that to the skies
  Thou didst bid the loved ones come.

VI.

Rest and peace for Jesus' sake!
  Father, at thy feet I kneel:
Bruiséd reeds thou wilt not break,
  Thou the broken heart wilt heal.

1882.

LIX.... 7's.

Then cometh Jesus with them unto a place called Gethsemane.
Matt. xxvi. 36.

I.

O THE agonizing prayer
　　Rising on the midnight air!
"Let this cup pass from thy Son:
Not my will, but thine be done!"
　　Jesus in Gethsemane!

II.

O the tears and bloody sweat
Falling fast on Olivet!
In thy lonely agony,
Shedding crimson tears for me,
　　Jesus in Gethsemane!

III.

O what wrath of earth and hell
On thy head unpitying fell,
When thy passion-time began,
Bearer of the sin of man,
　　Jesus in Gethsemane!

IV.

Sorrow none had ever known
Came upon thy soul alone:
While its billows o'er thee swept,
Near at hand thy followers slept,
     Jesus in Gethsemane!

V.

Waken me from sinful sleep:
Faithful, loving, make me keep,
Watching every hour with thee
Who didst agonize for me,
     Jesus in Gethsemane!

VI.

Crimson'd once, but beauteous now,
O what glory crowns thy brow!
All the world shall bend the knee,
Lord triumphant! unto thee,
     Conqueror in Gethsemane!

1883.

LX. .... 7's.

Casting all pour anxirtp upon him, because he careth for pou.
1 Peter v. 7.

I.

CAST thy burden on the Lord!
  Is this message meant for me?
May I take him at his word,
  And will he my helper be?

II.

In my daily household care,
  In the business of the day,
Will the Lord the burden bear
  Or his strength upon me lay?

III.

When the evil one shall cast
  Tempting baits to snare my soul,
Or shall taunt me with the past,
  Will the Lord his power control?

IV.

When the bitterness of grief
Shall upon my bosom prey,
Will he give me swift relief?
Will he take the pain away?

V.

When the parting hour is near,
Will his everlasting love
Conquer every doubt and fear
And the sting of death remove?

VI.

'Tis the promise of the Lord,
Meant for me on every day:
Heaven and earth may fail,—his word
Never once shall pass away.

1882.

LXI. . . . . C. M.

Behold, my servants shall sing for joy of heart.—Isa. lxv. 1.

I.

SOMETIMES, in quiet revery,
  When day is growing dim,
The heart is singing silently
  A sweet unwritten hymn.

II.

The strains are not to measure wrought
  By cunning of the mind,
But seem like hymnings angels brought
  From heaven, and left behind.

III.

The misty hills of bygone grief,
  Once dark to look upon,
Stand out like blessings in relief
  Against the setting sun.

IV.

The rain may fall, the wind may blow,
   The soul unhinder'd sings,
While, like the bird 'neath sheltering bough,
   She sits with folded wings,—

V.

A brief and pleasant resting space,
   A glance at Beulah land,
Before she girds herself apace
   For work that waits the hand.

VI.

Then, giving thanks to Him who pour'd
   Refreshment in her cup,
She hears the calling of her Lord
   And takes her labour up.

 1882.

LXII. . . . . C. M. P.

*And there shall be night no more; and they need no light of lamp,
neither light of sun.—Rev. xxii. 5.*

I.

O LAND of day, eternal day,
    Unbroken by a night:
No need of candle nor of sun
Thy blessed fields to shine upon,—
    The Lamb of God thy light.

II.

O land of life that cannot die,
    To mortals open'd up:
No more the drooping of the eye,
The parting word, the fitful sigh,
    The bitter-tasting cup.

III.

O land of rest and sweet content,
    The time of battle o'er,

The weary victors, laying down
The cross, receive from Christ the crown
   To wear forevermore.

IV.

O land of beauty, beautiful
   Beyond the brightest dream
Of poet in his time of power:
No painter in his happiest hour
   Has caught its faintest gleam.

V.

Lord of the land! Eternal King
   Of a domain so fair!
O give us grace to watch and wait,
On duty at the outer gate,
   Till we may enter there.

1877.

LXIII. . . . . 7, 6, P.

𝔄men: 𝔅lessing, anð glorg, anð wisðom, anð thanksgibing, anð honour, anð power, anð might, be unto our 𝔊oð for eber anð eber.—Rev. vii. 12.

I.

GLORY be to God on high!
　Glory in the highest!
Lord of wondrous majesty,
Maker of the earth and sky:
Saints redeem'd and angels cry,
　Glory be to God on high!
　Glory in the highest!

II.

　Glory be to God on high!
　Glory in the highest!
Father, Son, and Holy Ghost!
Praises in the uttermost
Earth shall sing with heaven's host:
　Glory be to God on high!
　Glory in the highest!

1883.

LXIV. . . . . 8, 8, 8.

𝔚𝔥𝔶 𝔰𝔢𝔢𝔨 𝔶𝔢 𝔥𝔦𝔪 𝔱𝔥𝔞𝔱 𝔩𝔦𝔟𝔢𝔱𝔥 𝔞𝔪𝔬𝔫𝔤 𝔱𝔥𝔢 𝔡𝔢𝔞𝔡? 𝔥𝔢 𝔦𝔰 𝔫𝔬𝔱 𝔥𝔢𝔯𝔢, 𝔟𝔲𝔱 𝔦𝔰 𝔯𝔦𝔰𝔢𝔫.—Luke xxiv. 5, 6.

I.

CHRIST is risen! O the wonder!
Rending bands of death asunder,
Rising to the glory yonder!

II.

Silently as morning breaking
Came the wonderful awaking,
Christ again his Godhead taking:

III.

In the stillness of the morning,
Angels heralding no warning,
Though the world's new light was dawning.

IV.

Ere sunrising, one came seeking,
She whose heart with pain was reeking,
Tears her pallid cheek bestreaking.

12*

V.

Last she saw him faint and dying;
Stark and cold her Lord was lying,
Ere she left him, weeping, sighing.

VI.

Lone she stood in tearful wonder:
Who had rent His tomb asunder?
Who so vile the grave to plunder?

VII.

She, amazed, her watch was keeping,
Blinding mists her vision steeping:
"Woman, why art thou a-weeping?"

VIII.

Was the startled woman chary?
Was she in her answering wary?
What a change when He said, "Mary!"

IX.

Once the piteous supplication,
Now the glad ejaculation,
"Master!" in rapt adoration.

X.

No more mocking, no more scourging,
Priest and mob the soldiers urging,
While the rage of hell was surging:

XI.

Crown of thorns no longer wearing,
Cruel taunts no longer bearing,
Nails no more his body tearing:

XII.

Majesty and gracious sweetness
Join in him with perfect meetness,
God and man in full completeness.

XIII.

Lord Jehovah! low before thee,
Ransom'd by thee, we adore thee:
Glory in the highest! Glory!

1882.

LXV. . . . . DIES IRÆ.

An attempt (based mainly on a literal rendering by J. Addison Campbell) to give in English verse the famous Latin hymn of Thomas of Celano, written in the thirteenth century.

I.

THE day of wrath, that certain day,
   In glowing embers earth shall lay,
Both David and the Sybil say.

II.

With trembling dread the world will quake
Or e'er the Judge shall inquest make,
And ruin all things overtake.

III.

The trump shall sound a startling tone
Throughout the graves of every zone,
And call all men before the throne.

IV.

And death and nature in surprise
Shall see the creature man arise
To answer at the dread assize.

V.

The written book will forth be brought,
With good and evil records fraught,
And man be judged for deed and thought.

VI.

When he shall sit upon his throne,
The Judge will make all secrets known;
Things unavenged there shall be none.

VII.

And what shall wretched I then plead?
Who then for me will intercede,
When e'en the just will mercy need?

VIII.

King of tremendous majesty,
Who sav'st thine own by grace most free,
Thou fount of pity, rescue me!

IX.

Remember, Jesus kind, I pray,
For me thou gav'st thy life away:
Then do not lose me on that day!

X.

While seeking me, I wearied thee;
Thou on the cross redeemedst me:
In vain let not such travail be!

XI.

Just and avenging Judge, I cry,
Give me remission ere I die,
Before the reckoning-day comes nigh.

XII.

A culprit groaning with his care,
My face the blush for sin shall wear;
O God, the pleading suppliant spare!

XIII.

The Magdalene was forgiven,
And e'en the thief by thee was shriven;
Thou giv'st me also hope of heaven.

XIV.

My prayers, unworthy, do not spurn;
Thou who art good, in kindness turn,
Lest I in fire eternal burn.

XV.

Far from the goats' accursèd band
Keep me apart, and make me stand
Among the sheep at thy right hand.

XVI.

When the accursed go to their place,
When dies the furious flame apace,
Then call my name with words of grace.

XVII.

Prostrate and suppliant, I pray,
With spirit crush'd to ashes gray,
O care for me at my last day!

Upon that day of tearful eyes,
When from the embers he shall rise,
And culprit man wait thy decree,
O God, then pardon even me.

Kind Lord Jesus, ever blest!
Give to thy redeeméd rest.

Amen.

1382.

LXVI. . . . . 8, 7, 4.

A man had two sons; and he came to the first, and said, Son, go
work to-day in the vineyard.—Matt. xxi. 28.

I.

IN the vineyard of our Father
   Daily work we find to do;
Scatter'd fruit our hands may gather,
    Though we are but weak and few:
     Little clusters
Help to fill the basket too.

II.

Toiling early in the morning,
   Catching moments through the day,
Nothing small or lowly scorning,—
    So we work, and watch, and pray;
     Gathering gladly
Free-will offerings by the way.

III.

Not for selfish praise or glory,
  Not for objects nothing worth,
But to send the blessed story
  Of the gospel o'er the earth,
    Telling mortals
  Of our Lord and Saviour's birth.

IV.

Up and ever at our calling,
  Till in death our lips are dumb,
Or till—sin's dominion falling—
  Christ shall in his kingdom come,
    And his children
  Reach their everlasting home.

V.

Steadfast, then, in our endeavour,
  Heavenly Father, may we be;
And forever, and forever,
  We will give the praise to thee;
    Alleluiah!
  Singing, all eternity.

1845.

LXVII. . . . . 7, 6.

𝕮𝔥𝔢 morning stars sang together, and all the sons of 𝕲𝔬𝔡 shouted
for joy.— Job xxxviii. 7.

I.

THE morning stars were singing
    With joy when time began;
And heavenly peals were ringing
    When God created man:
The universe was swelling
    With jubilant delight,
While all to all were telling
    The Lord Jehovah's might.

II.

A higher song of glory
    Was sung in after-days,—
And shepherds heard the story,
    As angels hymn'd His praise,—
Of Jesus in a manger,
    God's well-belovéd Son,
Who came to save from danger
    A race by sin undone.

III.

A multitude of voices
    Have learn'd this holy song;
And earth with heaven rejoices
    To roll the sound along.
With saints and angels o'er us,
    Singing before the throne,
We join the gladsome chorus,
    Glory to God alone!

1846.

LXVIII. . . . . 8, 7, 4.

Wilt thou not from this time cry unto me, My Father, thou art
the guide of my youth?—Jer. iii. 4.

I.

FATHER! in my life's young morning,
　　May thy word direct my way :
Let me heed each gracious warning,
　　Lest my feet should go astray :
　　　　Make me willing
　　All its precepts to obey.

II.

Father! gentle is thy teaching;
　　Be a docile spirit mine :
Every day thy grace beseeching,
　　Let thy loving-kindness shine
　　　　Always on me,
　　And my heart be wholly thine.

III.

Father! let me never covet
    Things of vanity and pride:
Teach me truth, and may I love it
    Better than all else beside:
        Blessed Bible!
    May it be my heavenward guide.

LXIX. . . . . 7, 6.

I.

I THANK the Lord my Maker
    For all his gifts to me:
For making me partaker
    Of bounties rich and free:
For father and for mother,
    Who give me clothes and food,
For sister and for brother,
    And all the kind and good.

II.

I thank the Lord my Saviour
    Who came for me to die,
And bless me with his favour
    And fit me for the sky,—
That, all my sins out-blotted,
    By Jesus wash'd away,
I may be found unspotted
    When comes the final day.

III.

I thank the Lord for giving
    The Spirit of his grace,
That I may serve him living,
    And, dying, reach the place
Where Jesus in his glory
    I shall forever see,
And tell the wondrous story
    Of all his love for me.

1844.

LXX. . . . . H. M.

Thou makest the outgoings of the morning and evening to rejoice.
Thou visitest the earth, and waterest it: thou greatly
enrichest it with the river of God.—Ps. lxv. 8, 9.

I.

WHO bids the wind to blow?
    Who makes the sun to shine,
And flowers and grass to grow
    Around this path of mine?
Who makes these shady trees arise,
And spread their boughs beneath the skies?

II.

Who makes this brook, so bright,
    From earth's cold bosom spring,
And sparkle in the light,
    And sweetly, sweetly sing,
As if an angel lent his voice
To help the rippling stream rejoice?

III.

Who gave the airy bird
  Soft feathers and swift wings,
And taught it music-words
  To charm us when it sings?—
Say, little bird! who taught you how
To sing so sweetly on that bough?

IV.

O, 'tis our Father, God,
  Who gives us every thing:
The grass, the flowery sod,
  The brook, and birds that sing;
And all the blessings of this day
He sheds upon our happy way.

V.

How good is God! He gave
  His only Son to die,
Our souls from death to save,
  And fit us for the sky
O, let us bow, and serve him here
With gratitude and love sincere.

1842.

LXXI. . . . . 8, 7, 8, 4.

𝕿𝖍𝖞 𝖜𝖔𝖗𝖉 𝖎𝖘 𝖆 𝖑𝖆𝖒𝖕 𝖚𝖓𝖙𝖔 𝖒𝖞 𝖋𝖊𝖊𝖙, 𝖆𝖓𝖉 𝖆 𝖑𝖎𝖌𝖍𝖙 𝖚𝖓𝖙𝖔 𝖒𝖞 𝖕𝖆𝖙𝖍.
Ps. cxix. 105.

I.

BOOK of grace, and book of glory!
Gift of God to age and youth;
Wondrous is thy sacred story,
Bright, bright with truth.

II.

Book of love! in accents tender,
Speaking unto such as we;
May it lead us, Lord, to render
All, all to thee.

III.

Book of hope! the spirit sighing
Consolation finds in thee,
As it hears the Saviour crying,
"Come, come to me."

IV.

Book of peace! when nights of sorrow
　　Fall upon us drearily,
Thou wilt bring a shining morrow,
　　Full, full of thee.

V.

Book of life! when we, reposing,
　　Bid farewell to friends we love,
Give us for the life then closing,
　　Life, life above.

1843.

Psalms.

Ninety-Seventh Psalm.

L. M.

J EHOVAH reigns! Let earth rejoice;
And let the multitude of isles
Be glad, and sing with tuneful voice;
And nature's face be clad in smiles.

Though clouds and darkness from afar
Are round about his presence known,
Yet righteousness and judgment are
The habitation of his throne.

A fire before him goes, and burns
His enemies on every side;
His lightnings flash; and earth by turns
Beholds and trembles in its pride.

The hills before his presence melt,
　　Like wax before the furious flame;
His presence by the earth is felt
　　Who built her everlasting frame.

The heavens declare his righteousness,
　　The people all his glory see;
While they who serve the images,
　　And boast in them, confounded be.

Then Zion heard, and she was glad;
　　The daughters of Judea sang
Rejoicingly, and through the land
　　The praises of thy judgments rang.

For thou, O Lord! above the earth
　　Art high; thou art exalted far
Above the kings of mortal birth,
　　Though lofty their aspirings are.

Hate evil, ye that love the Lord,
　　For he preserves the saintly soul;
And every danger he will ward,
　　And save from wicked men's control.

On righteous men shall light arise,
　　Like morning breaking o'er the hills;

And hope shall kindle in their eyes,
   While holy mirth their bosom fills.

Rejoice, ye righteous, in the Lord!
   Give thanks before his presence now;
In memory of his faithful word
   And holiness, give thanks, and bow.

1853.

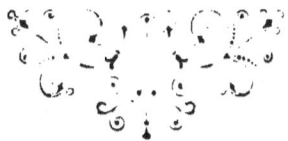

ONE HUNDRED AND TWENTY-FIRST PSALM.

6's.

I LIFT my longing eyes
    Up to the hills in vain:
Whence shall my help arise
    In time of want and pain?

My help is from the Lord
    Who gave all creatures birth,
And by his forming word
    Created heaven and earth.

No lurking enemy
    Thy foot shall turn astray,
For he that keepeth thee
    Will slumber not for aye.

Behold, he who in love
    Doth Israel ever keep,
His watchfulness shall prove,
    And slumber not nor sleep.

Thy keeper is the Lord,
   Jehovah is thy shade
On thy right hand : his word
   Thy sure defence is made.

By day the fervid sun
   Thy head shall never smite,
Nor shall the sickly moon
   Assail thee in the night.

Preserving thee from harm,
   All evil he'll control;
And his most gracious arm
   Shall e'er preserve thy soul.

When thou dost outward go,
   His grace shall go before;
In coming in also,
   Now and forevermore.

1871.

ONE HUNDRED AND FORTY-FIFTH PSALM.

C. M.

I WILL extol thee every day,
    My God, O glorious King;
And I will bless thy name for aye,
    Thy praise forever sing.

Great is the Lord and wonderful,
    And greatly to be praised:
His greatness is unsearchable,
    Beyond the heavens raised.

One generation, praising thee,
    Shall testimony bear
Unto the next, and wonderingly
    Thy mighty acts declare.

The honour of thy majesty,
    Thy wonders I'll proclaim;
Thine acts of terror men shall see
    And glorify thy name.

The memory of thy goodness they
    Shall utter far and wide;
Thy righteousness from day to day
    Shall sing on every side.

The Lord is gracious; full of kind
    Compassion: he is slow
To anger, and his holy mind
    Is great in mercy too.

The Lord our God is good to all,
    For all are in his thought;
His tender mercies richly fall
    On all that he hath wrought.

Thy works shall praise thee evermore,
    And thee thy saints shall bless;
Thy kingdom's glory and thy power
    To all the world confess;

Thy mighty acts that all may know
    Among the sons of men,
Thy kingdom's majesty to show
    To every creature's ken.

An everlasting kingdom's thine,
    And thy dominion sure

Throughout all generations' time
    Shall everywhere endure.

The Lord upholdeth all that fall,
    The bow'd with sorrow riven;
While on thee wait the eyes of all,
    Their meat is duly given.

Thou openest thy hand of grace,
    And thou dost satisfy
The wants of all in every place
    Who for thy presence cry.

The Lord is righteous in his ways,
    His works are holy all:
He's nigh to those that love his praise,
    And on him truly call.

The strong desire he will fulfil
    Of them that fear his name:
He hears their cry, and he will still
    Save them from harm and shame.

The Lord preserveth them from harm
    Who love him as their joy,
But wicked men his wrathful arm
    Will utterly destroy.

My mouth shall joyfully proclaim
    His praise from day to day:
Let all flesh bless his holy name
    Forever and for aye.

1871.

Doxologies.

L. M.

ALL praise to Thee, the triune One,
The Holy Father, Holy Son,
And Holy Spirit! Thou alone
Art King on the eternal throne.

C. M.

O HOLY, holy, holy Lord,
The Father and the Son
And Holy Ghost! Be thou adored
While endless ages run.

S. M.

BESIDE thee there is none:
Eternal God and King,
The Father, Son, and Holy Ghost,
Thy glorious praise we sing.

7's.

GLORY to thee evermore!
Glory in the uttermost!
Heaven and earth thy name adore,
Father, Son, and Holy Ghost.

7, 6.

THY love, O Holy Father,
  Thy grace, O Holy Son,
Thy peace, O Holy Spirit,
  Thy church abide upon:
While she her voice upraises
  To thy eternal throne,
And chants in endless praises
  Glory to God alone.

8, 7, 4.

GLORY in the highest! glory!
  Father, Son, and Holy Ghost:
King eternal! we adore thee,
    Singing with the heavenly host,
        Glory! glory!
  Glory be to God on high!

Finis.

ELECTROTYPED BY
MACKELLAR, SMITHS & JORDAN,
PHILADELPHIA,
PRINTED BY H. B. ASHMEAD.